Up to the Sky!

Written by Elizabeth A. Yoder
Illustrated by Darren McKee

Scott Foresman

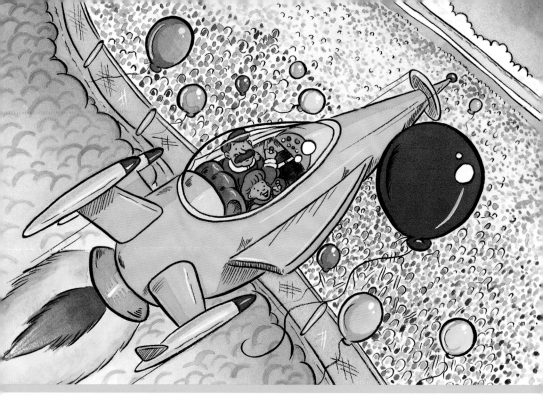

Fly, fly, up to the sky!
I see a balloon go by.

Fly, fly, up to the sky!

I see a bird go by.

Fly, fly, up to the sky!

Here is the blue Earth.

Fly, fly, up to the sky!

Here is the yellow moon.

Fly, fly, up to the sky!

Look at the stars.

We will fly by.

Fly, fly, up to the sky!

Look at the comet.

See it fly!

Down, down, down from

the sky! Here we are.

Now we say good-by!